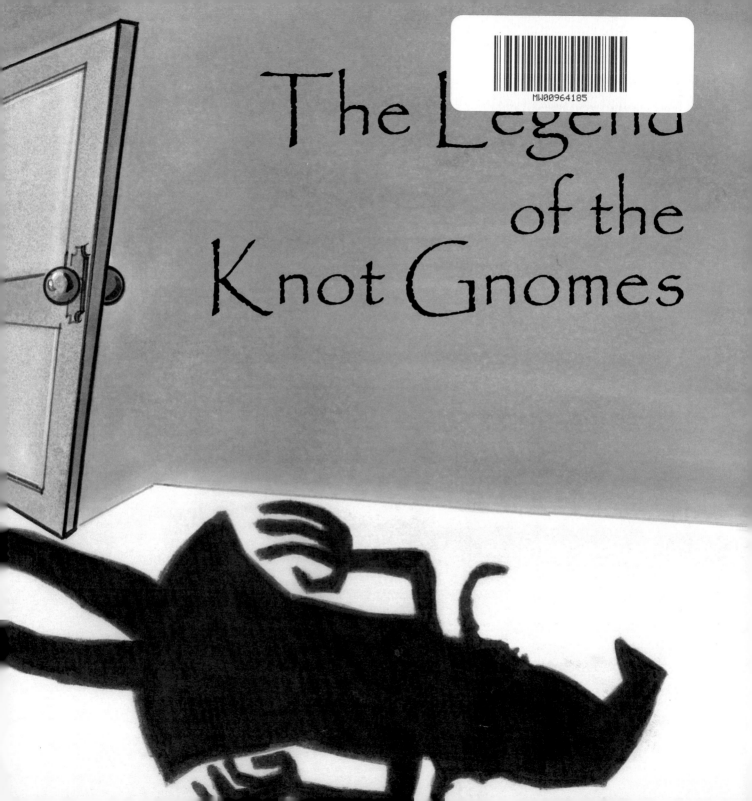

The Legend of the Knot Gnomes

To order additional copies of this book, contact:
Xlibris Corporation
1-888-795-4274
www.Xlibris.com
Orders@Xlibris.com

Dedicated to my daughter Madeline
who inspired the idea.

The Knot Gnomes

In the dark of the night
when all are asleep,
Knot Gnomes come creeping
with hardly a peep.

The Knot Gnomes like
to play in my hair.
This is unfortunately very unfair.

They twist it and jumble it
and make knotty knots.

They play jump
rope and games of
Knot Gnome
hopscotch.

Sometimes they chew gum
and it gets caught in my tresses,
making the biggest of gummy
gum messes.

All the time that
they play my hair gets
more entangled...

in unsolvable
knots that just
won't be wrangled.

The Knot Gnomes
keep playing
all through the night.
They show no signs
of stopping
'til dawn's early light.

When I awake in the morning
I look in the mirror.

There's not a thing I can do—
that much is clear.

Such a big
mucky mess,
it just
makes me . . .

SHOUT!!

My head is so full
of tangles and knots,
it'll take mommy
HOURS
to brush them
all out.

When my hair is finally brushed,
all shiny and clean,
I just know the Knot Gnomes
will be back tonight....